Paul Revere's Ride

A Level Three Reader

By Cynthia Klingel and Robert B. Noyed

The **Child's World®**

On the cover...
This drawing shows Paul Revere's ride.

Published by The Child's World®, Inc.

PO Box 326
Chanhassen, MN 55317-0326
800-599-READ
www.childsworld.com

Photo Credits
© Bettmann/CORBIS: 18, 26
© CORBIS: 9, 17, 25
© Hulton Archives: 22
© James P. Rowan: 6
© Photri, Inc.: 10
© Stock Montage: cover, 5, 13, 14, 21, 29

Project Coordination: Editorial Directions, Inc.
Photo Research: Alice K. Flanagan

Library of Congress Cataloging-in-Publication Data
Klingel, Cynthia Fitterer.
Paul Revere's ride / By Cynthia Klingel and Robert B. Noyed.
    p. cm.
ISBN 1-56766-960-3 (lib. bdg. : alk paper)
1. Revere, Paul, 1735-1818—Juvenile literature.
2. Statesmen—Massachusetts—Biography—Juvenile literature.
3. Massachusetts—History—Revolution, 1775-1783—Juvenile literature.
4. Massachusetts—Biography—Juvenile literature.
[1. Revere, Paul,1735-1818. 2. United States—History—Revolution, 1775-1783—Biography.]
I. Noyed, Robert B. II. Title.
F69.R43 K58 2001
973.3'311'092—dc21
                        00-013240

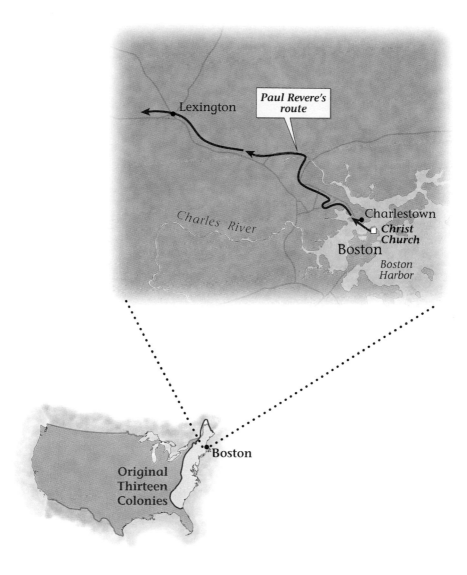

Do you know where Paul Revere's famous ride took place? Here is a map to help you find out.

Paul Revere was a great American. His famous ride warned **colonists** that the British were coming. He played an important role in the start of the Revolutionary War.

This is a painting of Paul Revere. →

Paul Revere was born and lived in Boston, Massachusetts. His family came to America from France. Paul's father wanted religious freedom. He was a **silversmith**. He made cups, bowls, and silverware and sold them to colonists.

Paul Revere learned how to be a silversmith from his father. Paul was only 18 years old when his father died. He earned money to take care of his mother and five brothers and sisters.

This painting shows Paul Revere working as a silversmith. →

Paul Revere also took a job ringing bells at Old North Church in Boston. This church is now called Christ Church. Paul rang the church bells three times a day. He also rang them to warn people about fires in the city.

← This is a statue of Paul Revere in front of Old North Church (Christ Church) in Boston.

When he was 15 years old, Paul formed a bell-ringing club. The members of the club learned how to play songs on the bells. They pulled thick ropes to ring each bell. They practiced for many hours.

Here you can see an ad for bells made by Paul Revere. ➔

Paul Revere & Son,

At their BELL *and* CANNON FOUNDERY, *at the*
North Part of BOSTON,

CAST *BELLS*, of all fizes ; every kind
of Brafs ORDNANCE, and every kind of
Compofition Work, for SHIPS, &c. *at the fhorteft notice :*
Manufacture COPPER into Sheets, Bolts,
Spikes, Nails, Rivets, Dovetails, &c. from *Mal-*
leable Copper.

They always keep, by them, every kind of
Copper faftening for Ships. They have now on
hand, a number of Church and Ship Bells, of different fizes ; a large quantity of Sheathing Copper,
from 16 up to 30 ounce : Bolts, Spikes, Nails, &c
of all fizes, which they warrant equal to English
manufacture.

Cafh and the higheft price given for old Copper and Brafs ·   march 20

When Paul was growing up, England controlled the 13 American **colonies**. Paul grew to dislike the British. He did not like the taxes that the British were charging the colonists. Paul joined a **militia** when he was 21 years old.

← This woodcut was made by Paul Revere. It shows British ships in Boston Harbor.

After the militia, Paul returned to his silversmith business. He was very successful. But British taxes soon made business difficult. Many people could no longer afford to buy his silver. Business slowed down.

This portrait of Paul Revere shows him holding a piece of silverware. →

Paul Revere became angry with the British. He joined with other young men in Boston to complain. These men called themselves the Sons of Liberty. John Hancock and Samuel Adams were members. The Sons of Liberty talked about being free from the British.

← This painting shows John Hancock, a member of the Sons of Liberty.

Paul Revere often took messages from the Sons of Liberty to other towns. He made cartoons making fun of the British. Paul drew a picture of the British attack called the Boston Massacre. He sold many copies of it. He used it to **rally** people against the British.

Paul Revere drew this picture of the Boston Massacre.

The BLOODY MASSACRE perpetrated in King——Street BOSTON on March 5ᵗʰ 1770, by a party of the 29ᵗʰ REᵍ

BUTCHERS HALL

CUSTOM HOUSE

Engrav'd Printed & Sold by PAUL REVERE BOSTON

ᵖᵖy BOSTON! see thy Sons deplore,
ᵃⁱlow'd Walks besmear'd with guiltless Gore:
faithless P—n and his savage Bands,
murd'rous Rancour stretch their bloody Hands;
ᶠierce Barbarians grining o'er their Prey,
ʳove the Carnage and enjoy the Day.

If scalding drops from Rage from Anguish Wrung
If speechless Sorrows lab'ring for a Tongue,
Or if a weeping World can ought appease
The plaintive Ghosts of Victims such as these;
The Patriot's copious Tears for each are shed,
A glorious Tribute which embalms the Dead

But know FATE summons to that awful G
Where JUSTICE strips the Murd'rer of his S
Should venal C—ts the scandal of the La
Snatch the relentless Villain from her Ha
Keen Execrations on this Plate inscri
Shall reach a JUDGE who never can be b

ᵗᵉ unhappy Sufferers were Messʳˢ Samˡ GRAY Samˡ MAVERICK, Jamˢ CALDWELL, CRISPUS ATTUCKS & Patᵏ C
Killed. Six wounded; two of them (CHRISTʳ MONK & JOHN CLARK) Mortally

In 1773, the Sons of Liberty protested the British tea tax. They went onto boats in the harbor and threw tea into the water. This protest was called the Boston Tea Party. Paul Revere was one of the men in this group.

← This drawing shows the Boston Tea Party.

Paul Revere often rode a horse to share messages. He is best known for his famous ride on April 18, 1775. Paul learned that the British army was coming on ships. He had two lights put in the **steeple** of Old North Church to warn people.

This painting shows Paul Revere's famous ride. →

Paul Revere left Boston in a boat. He landed across the harbor in Charlestown. He then borrowed a horse and rode through Lexington. He warned the colonists that the British were coming.

← Here you can see Paul riding to Lexington.

Paul Revere fought the British during the war. When the war was over, he returned to his silversmith business in Boston. Paul Revere's ride helped the colonists prepare to fight the British.

This drawing shows a soldier looking out for the British. →

29

Glossary

colonies (KOL-uh-neez)
Colonies are lands ruled by a
faraway country.

colonists (KOL-uh-nists)
Colonists are people who live
in a colony.

militia (muh-LISH-uh)
A militia is a group of people
trained to fight in times of
emergencies.

rally (RAL-lee)
To rally people means to bring
them together.

silversmith (SIL-ver-smith)
A silversmith makes or repairs
silver things.

steeple (STEE-pul)
A steeple is a high tower on
a church.

Index

To Find Out More

Books

Adler, David A. *A Picture Book of Paul Revere.* New York: Holiday House, 1995.

Gleiter, Jan, and Kathleen Thompson. *Paul Revere.* Austin, Tex.: Raintree/Steck-Vaughn, 1995.

Longfellow, Henry Wadsworth. *Paul Revere's Ride.* New York: Dutton Children's Books, 1990.

Web Sites

The Paul Revere House
http://www.paulreverehouse.org/justforkids/index.html
For information about Paul Revere's house and related activities for kids.

Home Page for Christ Church, Boston
http://www.oldnorth.com/
To visit the official Web site for Old North Church, now called Christ Church.

Note to Parents and Educators

Welcome to The Wonders of Reading™! These books provide text at three different levels for beginning readers to practice and strengthen their reading skills. In addition, the use of nonfiction text gives readers the valuable opportunity to *read to learn*, not just to learn to read.

These leveled readers allow children to choose books at their level of reading confidence and performance. Level One books offer beginning readers simple language, word choice, and sentence structure as well as a word list. Level Two books feature slightly more difficult vocabulary, longer sentences, and longer total text. In the back of each Level Two book are an index and a list of books and Web sites for finding out more information. Level Three books continue to extend word choice and length of text. In the back of each Level Three book are a glossary, an index, and a list of books and Web sites for further research.

State and national standards in reading and language arts emphasize using nonfiction at all levels of reading development. The Wonders of Reading™ books fill the historical void in nonfiction for primary grade readers with the additional benefit of a leveled text.

About the Authors

Cynthia Klingel has worked as a high school English teacher and an elementary teacher. She is currently the curriculum director for a Minnesota school district. Writing children's books is another way for her to continue her passion for sharing the written word with children. Cynthia is a frequent visitor to the children's section of bookstores and enjoys spending time with her many friends, family, and two daughters.

Robert Noyed started his career as a newspaper reporter. Since then, he has worked in communications and public relations for more than fourteen years for a Minnesota school district. He enjoys writing books for children and finds that it brings a different feeling of challenge and accomplishment from other writing projects. He is an avid reader who also enjoys music, theater, traveling, and spending time with his wife, son, and daughter.